DICK TRACY
on the Trail of the Blank

WALT DISNEY PICTURES presents

WARREN BEATTY

DICK TRACY

Original Score by DANNY ELFMAN

Editor RICHARD MARKS

Production Designer RICHARD SYLBERT

Cinematography by VITTORIO STORARO, A.I.C.-A.S.C.

Co-Producer JON LANDAU

Executive Producer BARRIE M. OSBORNE

Screenplay by JIM CASH & JACK EPPS, JR. and BO GOLDMAN & WARREN BEATTY

Produced and Directed by WARREN BEATTY

Soundtrack Album Available On Warner Bros. Records

Produced in association with
SILVER SCREEN PARTNERS IV

Dolby Stereo® Selected Theatres

Distributed by Buena Vista Pictures Distribution, Inc.

© 1990 THE WALT DISNEY COMPANY

Storybook adapted by ANDREW GUTELLE

Illustrated by FRED CARRILLO & DIANA WAKEMAN

A GOLDEN BOOK • NEW YORK
Western Publishing Company, Inc., Racine, Wisconsin 53404

It was a quiet night at the Club Ritz. Tomorrow the club would open again, and the tables would be packed with gamblers.

Piano player 88 Keys began to play the piano, and the beautiful Breathless Mahoney slowly walked onstage. She leaned on the piano and started to sing.

Big Boy Caprice had taken over the Club Ritz, and now he wanted to take over the City, too. In the club's conference room the toughest crooks in town were having a meeting. Sitting around Big Boy's table were Pruneface, Johnny Ramm, Spud Spaldoni, and many other kings of crime.

"Gentlemen, we've got a problem with organization," said Big Boy. "While we are divided, the cops, namely Dick Tracy, can keep us under control. But if we form a big company, with me as chairman of the board, together we will own this town."

The gangsters knew they wouldn't be safe unless Tracy was out of the way. What they didn't know was that the City's top crime fighter was watching them from the window.

The next morning Tracy was at home with a young orphan he and Tess Trueheart, his girlfriend, had found on the street. Now the Kid, as the boy called himself, was staying with Tracy until the detective could figure out what to do with him.

"Why don't you take me with you?" asked the Kid, who was watching Tracy get ready to leave. "I could be a big help to you."

"Forget it," said Tracy. "Most kids your age aren't even allowed to stay home alone, much less hang around with cops. I'll handle Big Boy myself."

That same morning, in a deserted part of town, 88 Keys met a mysterious villain who had no face. The piano player was nervous. "Why did you send for me?" 88 Keys asked.

"Give this letter to Big Boy," said the shadowy figure known as the Blank.

88 Keys brought the letter to Big Boy. It said, "For a share of your business, I will get rid of Dick Tracy."

Big Boy didn't want to make a deal. "I don't need some stranger moving in on my territory," he growled, "especially some bum no one's ever seen."

Later that night the Club Ritz opened. While Breathless Mahoney was singing, people were crowding the tables and gambling.

Outside, the police were gathered. With Tracy in the lead, they prepared to raid the club, but a man at the door spotted them. He alerted Big Boy's men to hide the gambling tables.

When Tracy and the police searched the club, they couldn't find any trace of gambling.

"Next time let us know when you're dropping in," said Big Boy, laughing. "We'll throw you a party!"

But what Big Boy didn't know was that Tracy had set a trap. Bug Bailey had sneaked into the club's attic and was using a microphone, dropped through a hole in the ceiling, to snoop on Big Boy. When the gangster planned a crime, Bug would be able to let Dick Tracy know.

It was the cops against the robbers, and the good guys were winning. Bug Bailey was using his wrist-radio to warn Tracy each time Big Boy's mob was on the move.

"Everywhere I turn I see Tracy!" Big Boy screamed. "It's like he's reading my mind!"

Big Boy needed help, so he took 88 Keys for a ride. When no one could see or hear them, he handed the piano player an envelope stuffed with money.

"OK," said Big Boy, "tell this Blank character to get rid of Tracy."

The Blank knew that Dick Tracy's weak spot was his love for his girlfriend, Tess Trueheart, so he kidnapped her.

On the night of the kidnapping the Blank lured Tracy to Tess's greenhouse with a note in Tess's handwriting. While waiting for his sweetheart, Tracy was smelling some flowers when all of a sudden his knees started to shake and the room seemed to be spinning. Tracy struggled to keep his balance.

"Just relax and smell the gas," said the Blank as he started to walk outside. "You're going to sleep."

BANG! BANG! Two loud shots rang out, and Tracy woke up. He was in a strange room and had been asleep for hours. Lying on the floor was another man. Someone had shot him, and Tracy was holding a gun. Just then the police rushed into the room.

"Where am I?" Tracy asked.

"You're in the Midway Hotel," said a police officer, handcuffing Tracy. "And you're under arrest for shooting District Attorney Fletcher."

That night Tracy was handcuffed again. He was being moved to County Jail. But when he got inside the police car, Tracy looked up to see his buddies Sam Catchem and Pat Patton, fellow police officers, in the front seat.

Sam unlocked Tracy's handcuffs. "We have eight hours before you have to be at the jail," he said. "A smart detective like you ought to be able to solve a case in that time."

Meanwhile, at the Club Ritz, Big Boy was holding court. Other gang lords and their bodyguards were enjoying themselves at the gambling tables. Big Boy had discovered Bug Bailey and had him taken to the Southside Warehouse. With Tracy out of the way, too, there was nothing stopping the gangsters from taking over the City.

But Flattop had found Tess Trueheart tied up in the attic. He came rushing in to tell Big Boy, who ran upstairs.

"We've been tricked!" said Big Boy. "They're going to get us for kidnapping. Take this dame out of here before the cops show up!"

But it was too late. The club was surrounded by police. While his men rushed outside, guns blasting, Big Boy grabbed Tess and tried to escape. He opened a secret door in the cellar and disappeared into a tunnel that led to the river.

Just as Big Boy was dragging Tess across a drawbridge, it started to open. He turned around and saw Dick Tracy heading for him. He ran into the gear house, pulling Tess with him.

"You've lost, Big Boy," said Tracy.

Big Boy pointed his gun at Tess, who was tied to the gears. "Drop your gun, copper," he said, "or this next bullet has your girlfriend's name on it."

Dick Tracy dropped his gun, but it went off when it hit the ground. For a moment Big Boy was confused, and he took his eyes off the detective, who jumped at him.

Big Boy fought fiercely, but Tracy knocked him to the ground with a powerful punch.

As Tracy moved to free Tess he saw a figure in the background. The Blank had appeared and was pointing a gun at them.

"Don't move," said the Blank. "I've won. With Big Boy Caprice *and* Dick Tracy out of the way, I'll own this town."

Tracy turned toward the Blank, who paused for a moment and then began to squeeze the trigger.

Suddenly another figure came running into the gear house—the Kid.
He tackled the Blank from behind and knocked the villain's gun away.
Tracy untied Tess, then he went over to the Blank.
"It was a great plan, Blank," said Tracy. "It almost worked."
"Yeah," grumbled the Blank. "My only mistake was you."

After the police arrived, Tracy, Tess, and the Kid went off to Mike's Diner to celebrate. The case had been solved.

"I'm gonna be the greatest detective!" said the Kid, smiling. And Dick Tracy and Tess Trueheart had to agree.